To **Olivia**

The star of the story!

From

Olivia was VERY excited as it was the day before Christmas Eve, and everyone was rushing around getting everything ready for the celebrations ahead.

Cards had been posted,
twinkly lights had been put
up and Christmas trees
had been decorated.

There was also another
special event taking
place on this busy day -
the Christmas baking competition!
Tasty goodies of all kinds would be judged,
with the VERY BEST declared the overall winner!

6

This year's very important judge was Mrs Claus, who had been flown in by Rudolph on Santa's sleigh.

7

All the bakers were busy making their goodies.

There were mince pies, yule logs, festive cake, scrumptious puddings and of course Christmas cookies.

Olivia, who was on Santa's nice list and had been specially invited to watch the baking competition, noticed that one of the contestants, a little gingerbread girl, was crying.
"Hello, what's the matter?"
Olivia asked kindly.

The gingerbread girl sobbed to Olivia that she was ready to decorate her gingerbread cookies but that all her icing, raisins and chocolate buttons had gone MISSING! "Don't worry," Olivia gently told the gingerbread girl. "I will help you to look for them."

The gingerbread girl jumped for joy, then pointed to the clock on the wall. They didn't have much time as Mrs Claus would soon start the judging.

11

Olivia began to look for clues - perhaps one of the other bakers had hidden the decorations!

They looked in Big Bear's back pocket.

They looked under Happy Hare's hat.

They even looked behind Eager Elf's ears, but the decorations were nowhere to be found!

Then, just as they were about to give up, clever Olivia noticed a little trail of icing sugar on the floor leading to the back door and it had some very strange-looking footprints in it!

13

They followed the footprints
and as they stepped outside they saw
some icing splats and blobs, and a few
raisins that had been dropped.

"Can you hear that?" Olivia asked the gingerbread girl.

There was a loud crunching followed by an even louder munching sound coming from Santa's sleigh.

15

Chewing on a crunchy carrot while singing some rather out of tune Christmas songs was Rudolph - and he was busily decorating reindeer shaped cookies with the missing decorations!

"Rudolph, what are you doing?" exclaimed Olivia. "The gingerbread girl needs those decorations!"

Rudolph explained that he just wanted to borrow them so he could enter the competition himself.

"I have a brilliant idea!" said Olivia. "You can help us decorate the cookies."

They all rushed back into the hall to get started as time was running out.

19

Icing, chocolate buttons and raisins flew everywhere as one by one the tasty gingerbread cookies were decorated and finished in the nick of time.

The three looked on nervously as Mrs Claus came to the table to inspect all the entries.

20

Then to their complete surprise she announced that Olivia, Rudolph and the gingerbread girl were the winners... and to Rudolph's dismay the first prize was a trip in Santa's sleigh!

The end

COLOR
ME IN